This igloo book belongs to:

....

igloobooks

Published in 2022
First published in the UK by Igloo Books Ltd
An imprint of Igloo Books Ltd
Cottage Farm, NN6 0BJ, UK
Owned by Bonnier Books
Sveavägen 56, Stockholm, Sweden
www.igloobooks.com

0122 002
2 4 6 8 10 9 7 5 3
ISBN 978-1-80022-656-2

Written by Melanie Joyce
Illustrated by Xenia Pavlova

Cover designed by Jason Shortland
Interiors designed by Kerri-Ann Hulme
Edited by Natalia Boileau

Printed and manufactured in China

Best Friends Forever

igloobooks

When Little Bear moved to a new house,
he missed his friends, **Badger, Bunny** and **Mouse.**
To make Little Bear feel better,
Mummy said, "Write them a letter."
Little Bear wrote...

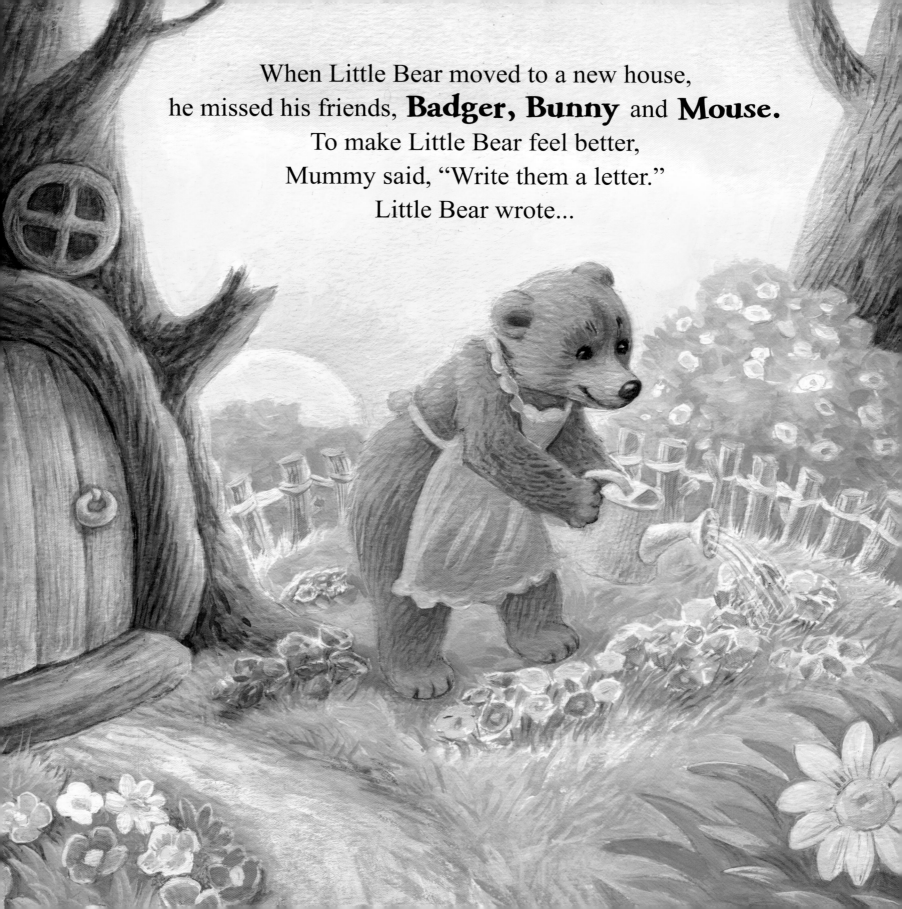

'Mouse, I miss your squeak.
Badger, I miss your giggles.
Bunny, I miss the way your nose wiggles.
I hope that you all miss me, too.
That's why I'm sending this letter to you.'

Swoosh! A rough wind blew.
It snatched the letter and away it flew.
"Give it back!" Little Bear cried.

SWOOSH!

But he **couldn't** catch the letter, however hard he tried.

Mummy felt **very** sorry for Little Bear.
She **hugged** him tight and said, "There, there."

WHOOSH!

The letter **blew** all around, then landed by Badger on the ground.

Badger opened the letter from Little Bear
and read all the **lovely** words written there.

"Bunny!" called Badger.
"I've got something to show you."

Bunny read the letter and wrote some words, too.

'Hello, Little Bear, it's Bunny.
I miss you because you're
cuddly and funny.'

Bunny and Badger ran to see Mouse.
They **tapped** on the wooden door of his house.
Mouse read the letter and wrote some words for his friend.

'I hope that our friendship will never end.'

When he had finished, Mouse **twiddled** his tail.
He said, "Let's send this
letter through the mail."

But Stork and the mailbag were flying away.
"Oh, no," said Bunny.
"We've missed the mail today."

"Come on," said Mouse.
"Let's deliver the letter to Little Bear's house."
He got a compass and some **tasty** snacks
and put them into little backpacks.

Mouse and his friends were ready to go.
"Which way is Bear's house? Does anybody know?"
On the way, they saw **Squirrel** in a tree.

"I know the way," he said. "Follow me."

They went **up** a hill and **down** to the bottom.
"Where now?" asked Mouse, but Squirrel had forgotten.

They had to walk a **long** time that day,
until they met **Fox** and asked him the way.

Fox wasn't sure, so he called to Bird.
"Do you know where Little Bear's
house is? Have you heard?"

"Yes," chirruped Bird. "Come with me."
And she **flew** off towards a big, old tree.

There was **Little Bear** who couldn't believe his eyes.
"Hello," said Bunny, Badger and Mouse. "Surprise!"

Little Bear read the letter and it made him **smile.**
"Thank you," he said. "Please stay for a while."

"I want to play with all of you.
Now I've got old friends and new ones, too!"

When Little Bear's friends went home,
he didn't feel sad or all alone.
His friends wrote letters **every** day.
So, he didn't feel bad about moving away.

Little Bear thought his friends were **very** clever.
He had no doubt at all they would be best friends **forever!**